CALICO ILLUSTRATED CLASSICS

Howard Pyle's

# King Arthur and the
# Knights of the Round Table

ADAPTED BY: Lisa Mullarkey
ILLUSTRATED BY: Howard McWilliam

magic
wagon

visit us at www.abdopublishing.com

Published by Magic Wagon, a division of the ABDO Group, 8000 West 78th Street, Edina, Minnesota 55439.

Printed in the United States of America, Melrose Park, Illinois.
102009
012010

 PRINTED ON RECYCLED PAPER

Original text by Howard Pyle
Adapted by Lisa Mullarkey
Illustrated by Howard McWilliam
Edited by Stephanie Hedlund and Rochelle Baltzer
Cover and interior design by Abbey Fitzgerald

**Library of Congress Cataloging-in-Publication Data**

Mullarkey, Lisa.
  King Arthur and the Knights of the Round Table / adapted by Lisa Mullarkey ; illustrated by Howard McWilliam ; based upon the works of Howard Pyle.
      p. cm. -- (Calico illustrated classics)
    ISBN 978-1-60270-707-8
    1. Arthurian romances--Adaptations. [1. Arthur, King--Legends. 2. Knights and knighthood--Folklore. 3. Folklore--England.] I. McWilliam, Howard, ill. II. Pyle, Howard, 1853-1911. King Arthur and the Knights of the Round Table. III. Title.
    PZ8.1.M89645Ki 2010
    398.2--dc22
                                                2009036524

# Table of Contents

# CHAPTER 1

# A Secret Birth

In ancient days, there lived a noble king named Uther-Pendragon. No one was as courageous, fair, or beloved at the time. With the help of his two advisors, he was a great ruler.

One of his advisors, Merlin, was a powerful enchanter and a great prophet. Sir Ulfius, his second advisor, gave him advice in battle. With their help, Uther-Pendragon was able to overcome all of his enemies. He became the king of England.

After Uther-Pendragon ruled for many years, he took a noble wife, Igraine. She had been married once before to Gerlois, the Duke of Tintegal. With the Duke of Tintegal, she had two daughters. One was Margaise and the other was Morgana le Fay, who became a famous sorceress.

After Gerlois's death, Igraine married Uther-Pendragon. He loved her children as if they were his own. Soon after they were married, Uther-Pendragon and Igraine were to have a son.

Merlin came to Uther-Pendragon with a warning. "Lord, in the near future, thee will become sick and die. Your child will be in great danger. Many enemies will try to kill him to prevent him from becoming our next ruler. Please permit Sir Ulfius and myself to hide him until he can guard himself from such dangers."

Uther-Pendragon replied, "I shall face death bravely and with cheerfulness if that's what is planned for me. As for my child, if thy prophecy is true, then the danger is great. Thou must take him to a safe place. He will be the most precious gift that I leave this land."

On the day the baby was born, Igraine wrapped him in blankets and placed him in a cradle made of gold. He was beautiful and strong. That evening, Merlin and Sir Ulfius whisked the child away.

Shortly after, Uther-Pendragon died as Merlin predicted. Then, the entire kingdom fell into chaos. There was much fighting and death. Traveling became impossible. Those who dared to travel were snatched and held for ransom. If ransom couldn't be paid, death would befall them. The land groaned with trouble.

Nearly eighteen years passed with this upheaval. Finally, the Archbishop of Canterbury summoned Merlin.

"Merlin, thou are the wisest man in all the land," the archbishop said. "Will peace ever be ours again?"

Merlin replied, "This country will soon have a king wiser than Uther-Pendragon. He shall bring peace and order where war and disorder exist. He will have King Uther-Pendragon's full royal blood."

This made the archbishop happy. "How shall we know the real king?"

So it came to be that Merlin used his magic. He made a huge marble stone appear before the cathedral door. Upon this block of marble stood an anvil. Into this, he thrust a sword. In letters of gold near the sword these words appeared:

*Whoso Pulleth out this Sword is by*

*Right of Birth King of England.*

As Christmas approached, Merlin asked the archbishop to call together the people of the land. He would then ask each man to draw out the sword. The man who succeeded would be the rightful king of Britain.

Christmas fell upon them. It seemed as if the entire world descended upon London.

"There are so many wise and great noblemen here," the archbishop worried. "What if we don't find anyone worthy of being the king of this realm?"

"Fear not, my Lord," said Merlin. "We will not find him among those we think are extraordinary and worthy. It is among those that are unknown that we shall find the one that is entirely worthy."

With the arrival of so many noblemen, the archbishop proclaimed that there should be a tournament. It would take place in a field three days before the men would be asked to remove the sword from the stone. All knights who were of noble blood were asked to partake in this tournament.

Sir Ector of Bonmaison, named the Trustworthy Knight, made his way to London with his two sons. The elder was Sir Kay, an honorable and well-known knight of great valor. The youngest was eighteen-year-old Arthur.

Sir Ector led his sons to London and set up a pavilion. He hung his banner like all the other nobles. The sky was filled with fluttering flags that represented the most noble families.

Among the great lords who came was King Lot of Orkney. He had married King Uther-Pendragon's stepdaughter, Morgana le Fay. King

Urien of Gore, who wed the other daughter, Margaise, joined them.

Soon the day of the tournament arrived. With his father's permission, Sir Kay entered. He asked Arthur to be his squire-at-arms. During the first rounds of battle, no one had done better than Sir Kay. Although many were trampled upon their own horses, Sir Kay fought with ease. He conquered them all.

"Sir Kay," came a voice, "do battle with me."

Sir Kay turned to see Sir Balmorgineas. He accepted the challenge. It was a fierce battle— one that left Sir Kay's sword snapped in two.

Three knights saw Sir Kay's trouble and pulled him to safety. Arthur ran to Sir Kay and offered him wine. Sir Kay said, "Arthur, run to our pavilion and fetch me a new sword."

Arthur did as he was told. But when he got to the pavilion, he couldn't find a sword. He feared he would let his brother down. Then he remembered the sword he had seen by the cathedral and ran to it. Not seeing any guard in sight, Arthur leaped upon the rock and pulled the sword from the stone. It was his!

Arthur wrapped the sword in a cloak and ran back to the tournament. When Sir Kay unwrapped the cloth, he was speechless. He recognized the sword at once!

"Arthur," he finally said, "where did thee get this sword?"

# The Sword in the Stone

"Brother," said Arthur, "I will tell the entire truth. I couldn't find a sword in the pavilion. Fearing thee would lose thy battle, I remembered the sword at the cathedral. I pulled it out with ease. I wrapped it in my cloak and ran to give it to thee."

Sir Kay collected his thoughts. *My brother doesn't know the significance of what he's done. Why shouldn't I lay claim to his great feat and reap the glory?*

"Give me the cloak and the sword," commanded Sir Kay. "Tell no one what thou hast done. Keep it between us. Now go tell father to come here right away."

Young Arthur was completely unaware of what he had done and what it meant. He did as Sir Kay told him.

"Father, thee must come at once," Arthur told Sir Ector. "Kay needs thee to go straight away to our pavilion. I think he has something extraordinary to tell thee."

When Sir Ector arrived at the pavilion, he noticed that Sir Kay's eyes shone with a brightness never seen before. "What is the matter, son?"

"It is a wonderful matter," said Sir Kay. He took his father by the arm and led him to a table in the center of the pavilion. Upon the table lay the cloak, which Sir Kay unwrapped to reveal the sword's blade. It glistened with splendor.

Sir Ector gasped. "What do my eyes see?"

"It's the sword that stood embedded in the stone," said Sir Kay. "I beg of thee. Please tell me what this means."

Sir Ector replied, "First, tell me how thee came upon the sword."

"Sire, my sword broke in battle and I found this sword and pulled it out," Sir Kay replied.

Sir Ector wasn't sure if he should believe his ears. "If thee did indeed draw this sword out of the stone, then thee should be able to thrust it back inside the stone."

Sir Kay cried out, "Who could perform such a great miracle as that?"

Sir Ector raised an eye. "Such a miracle is no greater than the miracle that thee performed in pulling the sword out from where it was embedded. Whoever heard of a man who could draw forth a sword from a place but not thrust it back to where it came?"

Sir Kay worried that he wouldn't be able to complete the task. *If my brother can do it, surely I am just as worthy*, he thought. He wrapped the sword in the cloak again.

Sir Kay headed toward the cathedral with Arthur and Sir Ector. As much as he tried to plunge the sword back into the stone, he couldn't.

"It is an impossible task of which thee ask me to do," Sir Kay said.

"How could thee get it out," asked Sir Ector, "if thee cannot get it back in?"

Sir Kay remained silent.

Arthur stepped forward. "Father, it was I who drew the sword out of the stone. I believe I shall be able to put it back in."

So Arthur took the sword from his brother and leaped upon the marble stone. He thrust the sword into the anvil. It went straight into the center of the marble!

After he performed this miracle, he drew the sword out once again swiftly and easily. Then once again, he thrust it back into the stone as he had done before.

Sir Ector cried out, "What a miracle my eyes have seen!" He knelt down before Arthur.

Arthur was confused. "Why do thee kneel before me?" He trembled. "Please, Father, answer me!"

"I am not thy father, Arthur. Thee are of royal blood. The blood of kings flows through thy veins. The way thee handled the sword proves it," Sir Ector replied.

Arthur started to cry.

Sir Kay couldn't move. *Is my brother a king?* he thought. *Could this be true?*

"Don't be afraid, Arthur," said Sir Ector. "The time has come for me to tell thee the truth. Eighteen years ago, Merlin came to me. He showed me the ring of Uther-Pendragon as proof of his honorable intentions. He told me to meet Sir Ulfius that night.

"That evening, he presented me with thee. I was told to raise thee as my own and tell no one any differently. I did all that he asked. Until now, I have never known who thy father was. I suspected kingly blood, but now I know the whole truth. Only the son of Uther-Pendragon could draw forth the sword from the anvil as thou hast done."

Arthur cried out, "No, no, no! It can't be! I have lost my father! I would rather have my father than be king!"

Two men approached Arthur and the sword. Sir Ector recognized Merlin and Sir Ulfius at once.

"What cheer!" shouted Sir Ector. "This is the child thee brought to me eighteen years ago. He is now the rightful king."

Merlin smiled. "He shall become Britain's greatest and most famous king. Within him lies the hope and salvation of the realm. Many great knights of excellence will gather around him and perform marvelous deeds. His reign will be full of splendor and glory. All the people shall rejoice in his kinghood."

Sir Kay stood motionless. Merlin looked sternly at Sir Ector and Sir Kay and said, "Protect and guard Arthur for the next three days. Behold him as the apple of thy eye. For in thy possession thee have the peace that was once ours in this land."

When Merlin and Sir Ulfius left, Arthur kissed his father's hand. "Thee will always be my father until the end."

Arthur was true to his word. He called Sir Ector his father until five years later when death came to Sir Ector.

# CHAPTER 3

## The New King

By Christmas morning, thousands had gathered in front of the cathedral. All came to see the kings and dukes attempt to pull the sword from the stone.

A brilliant-colored canopy was erected above the sword and the anvil. A platform had been built around the marble stone. A throne for the archbishop was built high above the stone. In this, he could look down upon the men and assure fairness.

With the morning half gone, the archbishop took his seat upon the throne. Nineteen men came forward with hope that they would be the chosen one. Excitement filled the air.

At the sound of the trumpet, King Lot of Orkney stepped forward. He mounted the platform and saluted the archbishop. He laid his hands on the sword, bent his body, and drew upon the sword with all his might. The blade didn't move. He tried three more times, and each time he failed.

King Urien of Gore, Lot's brother-in-law, tried next. He too could not pull the sword out of the stone. After his defeat, King Fion of Scotland, King Pellinore, King Mark of Cornwall, and King Leodegrance of Cameliard stepped forward. All were defeated. Some were filled with anger. Others felt ashamed that they failed.

After all failed, a low murmur rose throughout the spectators. "How is this? If these kings and dukes failed, then who may hope to succeed?"

The kings and dukes approached the archbishop. "Does Merlin try to make thee appear foolish? This task is impossible. No one can pull this sword out. Did Merlin intend to bring shame to all of us?"

"Merlin would never mock us. Have faith," said the archbishop. "If no one appears before us by day's end, then I shall choose one of thee here to become our king."

At that moment, Merlin and Sir Ulfius entered the pavilion with Arthur, Sir Kay, and Sir Ector. It was Merlin's plan to keep Arthur out of sight until this moment.

The archbishop asked, "Merlin, who have thee brought here today and why?"

"I have brought the one who will remove the sword from the stone. He is the only one who can do it," Merlin replied.

"Which one is he?" asked the archbishop.

Merlin laid his hand upon Arthur's shoulder. "Lord, he is the true son of Uther-Pendragon and his lawful wife, Queen Igraine."

Everyone who heard Merlin speak gasped. They didn't believe him. The archbishop spoke, "Until now, no one knew Uther-Pendragon had a son."

"That is true, my Lord. I foresaw that Uther-Pendragon would die soon after the birth of his son. I also saw that the king's enemies would lay their violent hands upon the child for the sake of his inheritance. So, Sir Ulfius and I took the baby to the trustworthy Sir Ector. He protected him until Arthur was needed to protect this realm."

Sir Ector spoke, "What he says is true. Thee have my sacred word of honor."

The archbishop smiled at Arthur and nodded toward the sword. "Who here can deny words from such an honorable man? With the grace of God, go do thy duty."

Arthur walked to the marble stone and laid his hands upon the sword. He bent his body and drew the sword out with ease. He swung it above his head so that it flashed like lightning.

Then, he slid the sword smoothly back into the stone.

There was great rejoicing at the pavilion. Many of the dukes and kings were amazed that someone little more than a boy had succeeded at what they couldn't. Most were willing to acknowledge Arthur as their king after witnessing his task.

Others refused to acknowledge Arthur. Some felt Merlin and Sir Ulfius had used Arthur to gain power for themselves. The most bitter were King Lot and King Urien, who were brothers by marriage with Arthur.

The archbishop was angry. "He is thy king who will save our land. He has done what all of thee have failed to do. Honor him."

King Lot, King Urien, and a few bitter dukes left the pavilion. The others saluted Arthur and paid him court. Arthur repaid their kindness by giving each one a kiss on the cheek.

When Arthur left, great crowds followed him. The streets were flooded with well–wishers, for the chosen king of England was among them. Some wanted to touch Arthur and feel his greatness.

Arthur was full of great joy and gladness. It was as if his soul took wing and flew like a bird into the sky.

# The Black Knight

After ruling for some time, word reached King Arthur that an evil knight dressed in black forbid passage to anyone he encountered. Many knights were left for dead and shown no respect.

One day, King Arthur declared that he would go forth and punish the Black Knight and humble him with his own hand. Although the knights of his court tried to dissuade him, King Arthur knew he must stop the Black Knight.

With Merlin at his side, King Arthur set out upon his white warhorse. After riding through the forest for a while, they saw a violent river before them. It rushed through a dark and dismal glen. Beyond the river was a lawn of green grass where jousting occurred. Beyond that was a tall and forbidding castle. This must be the castle that Arthur was seeking.

Upon the far side of the stream, there was an apple tree. Amid the leaves hung many shields. Most were tainted with blood. All of the shields were from those who the Black Knight had defeated in combat.

"There must be a hundred shields in that tree," said King Arthur.

"Come tomorrow, may thy shield not be among them," replied Merlin.

The two rode on until they came to a sign hanging from the bridge. It read:

*Whoso Strikes This Shield*
*Does So At His Own Peril.*

Upon reading the words, the king struck a violent blow to the shield. The sound echoed back from the smooth walls of the castle.

To answer the blow, the gates of the castle were immediately lowered to reveal a knight in black armor. Even his horse was as black as night. He trotted forward on his horse and saluted King Arthur.

"Ha, Sir Knight," he said, "why did thee strike upon my shield? I must now take thy shield away from thee and hang it on my tree. Thee shall certainly suffer great pain and discomfort to thy body."

"I have come to protect my people," arthur replied. "It is not my shield thee will get. I have come to redeem all the shields thee have taken."

Each knight dressed his spear and called out to his warhorse. The two steeds rushed forth like lightning. The earth trembled as they met in the middle, crashing together like thunderbolts. Connecting with such violence, their spears burst into splinters.

King Arthur was amazed that he didn't overthrow his opponent. After all, he was the best knight in all of Britain. So when they met a second time in the middle, King Arthur spoke to the knight with a great amount of courtesy.

"Sir Knight, I do not know who thee are. But I do know that thee are the strongest knight I have ever met. I ask thee to get down off thy horse and fight me on foot."

"Never," the Black Knight replied. "I shall overthrow thee before I challenge thee on foot." He summoned his squires to bring forth new spears. King Arthur chose one while the Black Knight took the other. They each returned to their side of the field.

As before, each knight rushed his steed to the assault. Once again, each one's blow to the other caused their spears to splinter. King Arthur asked yet again to battle it out with swords. The Black Knight refused him. It wasn't long before two esquires appeared with two fresh swords.

On the third assault, King Arthur struck the Black Knight with such a violent blow that his spear burst into splinters. But this time, the Black Knight's spear did not break or splinter. Instead, it struck King Arthur so hard that it pierced his shield. King Arthur and his steed were cast violently backward.

King Arthur was hurt! However, he kept his footing upon the ground and ran over to the Black Knight. He caught the horse's reins and cried out, "Come down, Black Knight, and fight me with thy sword."

"That I will not do," said the Black Knight, "for I have overthrown thee. Give me thy shield so I may hang it upon my apple tree."

"I will not yield myself or my shield until thou has conquered me on the ground." King Arthur pushed the reins so hard the steed bucked. This sent the Black Knight to the ground.

Each knight was furious with the other and drew their swords. They rushed together like bulls in battle. They struck again and again. The sound of their blows filled the field. The

armor of both was filled with blood from the wounds that were given and received.

At last King Arthur struck a blow so fierce that no armor could protect the Black Knight. The Black Knight groaned and staggered. He ran about in a circle as though he had gone blind and knew not where to run. The blow was so strong that King Arthur's sword broke into three pieces.

Although in pain, the Black Knight regained his senses. Knowing his opponent had no sword, he began a merciless stroking of the air. His sword cut through King Arthur's shield and helmet and landed upon his head.

King Arthur believed he had received his death wound by the pain and blood. However, even when the Black Knight demanded he surrender his shield, King Arthur refused.

He lifted himself to his feet and grabbed the Black Knight by both arms. Then he placed his knee behind the thigh of the Black Knight.

King Arthur pushed the Black Knight as hard as he could and the Black Knight fell to the ground. King Arthur took off his opponent's helmet to find out who the black armor was hiding.

# The Black Knight Revealed

It was King Pellinore beneath the black helmet! He was King Arthur's old enemy.

"Pellinore? Is that thee? How can this be?" King Arthur held a dagger to his throat. "Now thee must yield thy shield to me. Thou are at my mercy."

King Pellinore did not want to yield to anyone. He knew that the knight before him was weak from his wounds. He had lost a lot of blood. So he grabbed Arthur's wrist, flipped him to the ground, and placed the dagger to his throat.

"Thou will yield thy shield to me just as I demanded before," Pellinore said. Then he raised the dagger above Arthur's head and prepared to kill him.

At this moment, Merlin rushed into the field. "Stop! Stop your foolish ways. He who lies beneath thee is King Arthur!"

King Pellinore's eyes grew wide. He removed Arthur's helmet. "It's true! King Arthur looks back at my face." He turned toward Merlin. "I've come eye to eye with the man who has destroyed me. The one who doomed me to death. He has taken my power, my kingship, and my estates. He has left me only this dismal castle." He raised the dagger higher. "He deserves nothing but death!"

King Pellinore had never felt such hatred for any one man. "I must kill him now with one final blow. If I let him go free, he will have revenge on me for the ill suffered at my hands." He thrust the dagger with full force at King Arthur's neck for the final blow.

"He does not deserve death. I shall save him." Merlin lifted his staff and struck King

Pellinore across the shoulders. King Pellinore fell down with his eyes closed as if he had taken his last breath.

King Arthur lifted himself upon one elbow. "What have thee done, Merlin? Thou hast used thy magic to kill one of the best knights in the world!"

"Not so, my lord King!" said Merlin. "Thou are closer to death than thy enemy. He's sleeping and will soon awake. But thee will die shortly if thy wounds aren't taken care of. Your wounds are grave. Deadly."

Indeed King Arthur was near death from the wounds he had received from Pellinore. Merlin hung the king's shield upon the horn of his saddle and helped King Arthur onto his horse. Leading the horse by the bridle, Merlin led him out of the forest in search of help.

Merlin brought King Arthur to the home of a holy hermit who was well versed in treating wounds. This place was well regarded among the nobles who brought their wounded to him.

Merlin and the hermit lifted King Arthur down from the saddle. They laid him upon a couch of moss and unlaced his armor. King Arthur lay for two days as the hermit tended his wounds.

It was upon the second day that Lady Guinevere of Cameliard and her court traveled to the holy man for help. Lady Guinevere had a favorite page who was sick with fever. She trusted the holy man. She knew he would cure him.

When Lady Guinevere arrived, she noticed the milk-white warhorse chopping at the grass. She looked around and saw Merlin standing by a door. "Whose warhorse is this and why is it here?"

Merlin replied, "Lady, it belongs to a knight who lies seriously wounded inside this door. He is near death."

"Pity of heaven!" cried the lady. "May I see the wounded knight?"

So Merlin led Lady Guinevere to the knight in the hermit's house without sharing his identity. When Lady Guinevere saw King Arthur, she gasped. Never before had she seen such a noble-looking knight!

Arthur gazed into Lady Guinevere's eyes. Although he was in a weakened state, he thought for sure she was an angel sent from above to visit him.

Lady Guinevere had a skilled doctor in her court who tended to Arthur's wounds. When he worked his charms, Arthur felt his aches disappear and his wounds heal.

By the time Lady Guinevere departed with her court three days later, King Arthur was almost entirely healed.

This was the first time that King Arthur ever saw Lady Guinevere of Cameliard. She was by far the most beautiful woman he had ever seen.

He prayed it would not be the last time he laid his eyes upon her. He pledged allegiance to her and promised to serve her faithfully. In time, he would be called upon to make true his promises to her.

# CHAPTER 6

## *Excalibur*

The recovered King Arthur had a strong desire to battle King Pellinore once more. "Merlin, I must fight King Pellinore again. He is by far the strongest knight I've encountered."

"Thee are indeed very brave, my Lord," said Merlin, "to have such an appetite for battle. But seeing that thee almost died four days ago, how will thee prepare for battle? Thee have no sword. No spear."

"I must find a weapon," said King Arthur.

Merlin announced, "There is a part of the forest which is enchanted. It is a wonderful land with a magical lake. At the center of that lake, a woman's arm appears. It holds a sword. Not just an ordinary sword but one called

Excalibur. It's so named after its marvelous beauty and brightness.

"All knights who've seen it have wanted it. However, not one has been able to obtain it. Whenever a man approached it, he'd sink into the lake or the arm disappeared. Come with me and thee shall see Excalibur with thy own eyes."

After walking a bit, they saw a white doe with a golden collar around its neck. "Let's follow that doe," said Merlin. "It will lead us where we need to go."

By following the doe, they were led to an opening in the trees. Beyond it, there was a small patch of grass. Upon this grass was a table topped with a feast. Standing near the table was a page dressed in green. The page greeted King Arthur and Merlin. "Welcome to this place. Please refresh thyself before traveling on."

Arthur wondered whether this might be an evil enchantment. "Thee are safe here," said Merlin. "Eat. Drink. This feast was prepared especially for thee."

Arthur and Merlin were served food upon silver plates and wine in golden goblets. After they had their fill, they continued looking for the enchanted lake.

About mid-afternoon, the two came upon a great plain. It was filled with more flowers than any man could count. The land appeared to be made of gold for it was so bright and beautiful.

Midway in the plain, a lake with water as bright as silver appeared. Around the lake was a splendid border of lilies and daffodils. There wasn't a single sign of human life. King Arthur knew it must be the enchanted land.

As he approached the water's edge, he saw the fair and beautiful arm. Just as Merlin had promised! The arm was covered in white cloth. It held a sword of marvelous workmanship high above the water.

King Arthur sat upon his horse and gazed at the motionless arm. "How will I get that sword from this deep lake?"

Just then he noticed a strange lady walking through the flowers. Dressed all in green with crimson and gold thread woven in her hair, she was a sight to behold. Around her neck hung a beautiful necklace of opal stones and emeralds.

King Arthur dismounted his horse and kneeled in front of the lady. "Lady, I do think thee must be a fairy. This land is so beautiful that only a fairy could live within."

The lady replied, "I am indeed a fairy, King Arthur. My name is Nymue. I am in charge of the Ladies of the Lake. My sisters and I have created a home beyond the lake. It is entirely hidden from sight. No mortal man may cross this lake or he will perish."

"Lady," said King Arthur, "I am afraid I've intruded upon the solitude of thy home."

"Not so, King Arthur. Thee are welcome here. I have a great friendliness for noble knights. Thee certainly are such. But I do ask, why are thee here?"

King Arthur explained how he had lost his

sword in a battle with King Pellinore. "Merlin told me about Excalibur. I do hope I'm worthy of it," King Arthur concluded

The Lady of the Lake smiled. "That sword is hard to achieve. Many knights have lost their lives trying to get it. But I'll help thee."

She lifted a single emerald necklace around her neck. The emerald was carved into a whistle. She placed it upon her lips and blew into it. A boat of carved brass appeared. It moved upon the water like a swan.

The Lady of the Lake told King Arthur to enter the boat. The boat lurched forth, leaving the lady and Merlin by the water's edge. The boat raced to the arm. King Arthur reached up to the arm and took the sword in his hand. The arm let the sword go then disappeared into the water.

King Arthur's heart swelled with joy. Excalibur was a hundred times more beautiful than he had thought possible! When he returned to shore, he thanked the Lady of the Lake for her help.

# The Sheath's Power

The next day, Merlin and King Arthur arrived at the valley of the Black Knight. Everything was exactly as they had left it. They saw the gloomy castle, the lawn of smooth grass, the apple tree covered with shields, and the bridge where the Black Knight's shield hung.

King Arthur rode his steed up to the shield and struck it with a blow. Immediately, the gate of the castle fell. The Black Knight rode forth on his horse with weapon in hand.

"Sir Pellinore, we now know each other well. We have our own opinions about each other. Thou feels I've driven thee to this forest and have taken away thy kingly state. But I believe thee has injured my people. This is unacceptable. So I challenge thee to fight me, man-to-man, until one of us has conquered the other."

The Black Knight bowed and took his place at the far end of the field. Just as before, the two men rode into the middle of the field and crashed together with thundering strength.

Once again, both spears splintered and were discarded. Each knight quickly jumped off his horse and drew his sword. They fell into fierce combat.

Having Excalibur, King Arthur quickly overcame his enemy. He gave the Black Knight several wounds. Yet he received none himself. Nor did he shed a single drop of blood.

At last, King Arthur delivered such a fierce blow that King Pellinore lost his sword and shield. His armor was stained crimson. He sank to his knees and pleaded with Arthur, "Spare my life and I will yield to thee."

"I will do more than spare thy life. I will restore thee to power. You shall have thy land once again. I bear no ill will toward thee. But I can have no enemies or rebels against me. He who is against me is against my people. And he who is against my people is against me.

"To show thy faith in me, send me two of thy sons. Thy youngest may stay with thee as a sign of my good faith in thee. Thy two oldest will serve as knights in my court." With that, King Arthur took Pellinore inside his castle and tended to his wounds.

The next morning, King Arthur and Merlin returned to the court. Arthur was in a splendid mood thinking about his victory and Excalibur. Not only had he defeated a bitter enemy and turned him into a friend, but he also obtained a sword—a sword which no man had been able to possess.

As they rode, Merlin asked, "My King, would thee rather have Excalibur or the sheath that holds it?"

Arthur answered immediately. "What a question! Ten thousand times would I rather have Excalibur."

"Thou are wrong, my Lord," said Merlin as he shook his head. "Excalibur is so strong that it can cut a bar of iron in two. That is true. But its sheath is of greater power. He who wears it can suffer no wound in battle nor lose a single drop of blood."

King Arthur's eyes told Merlin that he did not believe his words.

"It is true," assured Merlin. "Think to thy battle with Pellinore. Thou suffered no wound. No blood flowed from thy body."

King Arthur was angry. "Thou has taken my battle glory from me. What good is conquering an enemy if it's done by magic?"

"Keep in mind that thee are not an ordinary knight," said Merlin. "Thou are a king and thy life belongs to thy people. Thou must do all thee can to preserve it for them. Thou must keep that sword so it can safeguard thy life at all times."

King Arthur knew Merlin was wise. Once again, he bowed to Merlin's wisdom. "I'll keep both Excalibur and the sheath to preserve my life. Nevertheless, I'll never again use them in battle."

King Arthur remained true to his word. From that day forward, he used a lance on horseback.

# A King in Disguise

Upon his return, King Arthur proclaimed a high feast. A majestic court gathered at his castle. After the feast, a messenger came from the West Country.

"Greeting to thy king!" said the messenger.

"Speak to me," said King Arthur. "What is thy message?"

"I come from King Leodegrance of Cameliard, who is in trouble. Thy enemy, King Ryence of North Wales, makes demands of my master. King Leodegrance does not wish to meet his demands. Since thee brought peace to this realm, King Leodegrance has no knights to protect him."

King Arthur, filled with peace and harmony only minutes before, became angry. "Tell me, what has King Ryence demanded of thy master?"

"He wants my master to give him land that borders North Wales. He also demands that Lady Guinevere, the king's daughter, be delivered in marriage to Duke Mordaunt. The duke is kin to King Ryence." The messenger continued, "The duke has a violent temper and is evil in appearance."

King Arthur's face flamed like fire and he ground his teeth together. He rose from his chair and tried to collect his thoughts. He was full of rage. He had loved Lady Guinevere ever since she appeared before him like a shining angel at the hermit's house. He'd never allow the duke her hand in marriage.

"Merlin, travel with me," Arthur ordered. "Sir Ulfius and Sir Kay, gather a large army and bring them to the royal castle of Tintagalon. It lay near the border of North Wales."

The men were met with cheers and well wishes as they left the castle. The people loved him dearly. It was in the castle's garden that King Arthur spoke freely to Merlin.

"I do believe that Lady Guinevere is the fairest lady in all the world. My heart is filled with love for her. No matter what I do, I think of her. This has been true since I first saw her standing over me a month ago. I will not allow any other man to have her for a wife."

Merlin remained silent, allowing the king to speak from his heart.

"Now I know thee well, Merlin. Thy magic may change a man's appearance so that those who know him best will not recognize him. I want thee to disguise me so I can go into Cameliard and see what peril King Leodegrance faces."

"If that is what thou desire, I shall disguise thee." Merlin gave King Arthur a little cap. It would disguise him as a poor boy when placed upon his head. He hid his golden collar and its jewel, which he always wore, with peasant clothes.

Fully disguised, King Arthur set out on foot to the town of Cameliard. From the moment he entered the castle, no one knew who he was.

When the head gardener saw how strong and tall he was, he made him a gardener's boy. King Arthur was very glad to be in that garden, for Lady Guinevere walked in it each day.

One morning in that first week, one of Lady Guinevere's attendants, Mellicene, rose early. She peered out the window to the flower garden below and saw a wonderful sight! A strange knight was sitting beside the fountain bathing his face in the cool water. His hair and beard were the color of red gold. Around his neck, she saw a golden collar that flashed in the sunlight.

Mellicene was mesmerized by his beauty. After wondering if she were dreaming, she ran down the stairs toward the fountain. She longed to see this knight up close.

King Arthur had heard the commotion as she entered the garden. He quickly put his cap back on. When Mellicene saw only a gardener's boy by the fountain, she looked confused.

"Who are thou?" she asked. "Where is the knight who was here?"

"I am the gardener's boy who came here to work. I've been here alone."

Mellicene didn't know what to believe. She didn't believe this boy, yet how could she not believe him? There was no one else in the garden.

"If thou deceives me, I shall whip thee." She turned and went away to tell Lady Guinevere all that she had seen.

Lady Guinevere laughed and mocked Mellicene. "Thou were dreaming!"

Mellicene started to believe that it must be the case. Still, she looked down to the garden each morning hoping to see the knight again.

Mellicene did see him again! This time, she brought Lady Guinevere to the window to see the great knight for herself! Beside him lay a collar of gold with jewels of many colors. When they ran to the fountain, they saw no knight. Only the gardener's boy! King Arthur had donned the cap just in time.

"Lady, no one has been here but me. I'm just a gardener's boy."

"Why do thee mock me?" asked Lady Guinevere. "Do gardener boys wear collars of gold? She grabbed the collar he had forgotten to put back on. "I have a mind to whip thee, but I'll refrain. Take the collar back to the knight to whom it belongs." She left.

Later that day, an idea came to Lady Guinevere. "Mellicene, go fetch the gardener's boy. Tell him I want a basket of fresh roses."

When a disguised King Arthur entered the room, Lady Guinevere spoke. "Take off thy cap in the presence of royalty."

"Lady, I cannot take it off. I have a sore upon my head."

When he came forward to deliver the roses, Lady Guinevere snatched the cap off his head. Some of the ladies shrieked. Others stared, not knowing what to do. But not one of the ladies knew it was King Arthur before them.

However, Lady Guinevere knew at once it was the knight she had nursed back to health. She laughed and flung his cap back at him.

"Take it and go away at once," she said. "Indeed a sore upon thy head!"

King Arthur backed out of the room the same way he had come, disguised as a gardener's boy. From then on, whenever she saw him, she would say in a loud voice, "Look! It's the gardener's boy with a sore on his head. He must wear a cap to cover the ugliness."

She mocked him openly. But in private, she made her ladies promise to tell no one what had happened.

# The White Champion

Duke Mordaunt and King Ryence rode to the castle with their knights. They pitched their pavilions in the meadows for all to see. Duke Mordaunt demanded Lady Guinevere's hand in marriage.

The duke rode up and down the castle walls. "Is there no one to come forth and battle me? How will thee fend off the knights of North Wales if thee are afraid to meet just one single knight in battle?"

No one dared to come forth. The people of Cameliard felt great shame and sorrow. King Arthur heard of the challenge. He finally had enough and laid his garden spade down. He secretly went to town, took off his cap, and sought out a merchant.

"Sir Merchant," said King Arthur, "I am a great friend of King Leodegrance. I wish him the best. Thee must be aware that the Duke of North Umber rides up and down the king's castle. He challenges all to fight him on behalf of Lady Guinevere. It is my hope that I shall fight him and uphold the honor of Cameliard."

The merchant saw King Arthur's signet ring. Although he didn't know who he was, he understood that he was of noble blood.

"I am in great need for the best armor thee have if I wish to defeat the duke. Thee have my word that I shall repay thee for thy troubles."

The merchant replied. "Even if thou were not of noble blood, I would give the armor to anyone who wants to rid us of the duke." He rang a little silver bell. At once, several attendants arrived and prepared the best weapons for the king.

They dressed Arthur in Spanish armor that was inlaid with gold. It was the best armor in the land. They handed him a shield of white and led him to the courtyard. A noble steed awaited him. The horse was milky white. The bridle and reins were studded with silver.

When the king rode away in his white and glittering armor, he looked like the full moon in harvest season. As he galloped to the castle, the townspeople turned and gazed after him. For he looked quite noble as he passed through the town.

Once King Arthur made it to the back entrance of the castle, he dismounted and tied his horse. He walked to the garden and asked to see Lady Guinevere.

When she came to the window above, King Arthur spoke, "Lady, I have great will to honor thee. I will go forth in combat with the Duke of North Umber and cause his downfall. Please give me some token to wear in battle so I can honor thee."

"Sir Knight, I wish I knew who thou were, but I will gladly give thee anything thy wish."

"I would like thy necklace to tie about my arm. It will give me strength in battle."

Lady Guinevere took off her necklace and dropped the pearls to King Arthur. King Arthur tied it around his arm and saluted Lady Guinevere. Then he went forth to fight.

By this time, word had spread that a great knight was to fight the Duke of North Umber. Great crowds gathered on the walls.

The gates to the castle opened and the bridge fell. The White Champion rode forth to face the duke. The duke gazed upon the man dressed all in white.

"Thou have no crest on thy shield," the duke said. "I don't know who thee are. I believe thou are a strong and courageous knight. But know that I will strike thee down from thy horse. Thou will not rise again."

King Arthur replied, "That shall be the will of heaven, not thy will."

The two saluted and each departed to their corner to prepare their spears. Silence fell upon the castle. Finally, each man shouted to his horse and launched forth in great battle. They met in the middle of the field with the noise of thunder.

The duke's spear splintered, but King Arthur's didn't. This sent the duke whirling into the air before landing with a thud on the ground.

King Arthur was victorious! He rode away from the castle, but he did not return to Cameliard or return his horse and weapons. He felt that the enemy was not yet done with him.

As King Arthur rode away in search of the knights of his court, he didn't think grand thoughts. Instead he asked, "What more may I do to make the world better because of my adventures?"

# CHAPTER 10

## The Duke's Downfall

The following day, Duke Mordaunt recovered from battle. Once again, he appeared in armor before the castle. His heart raced and his voice was angry.

"King Leodegrance, just because I suffered a fall from my horse does not mean I'll give up my demands," he declared. "Tomorrow I shall appear here with six companions. Bring seven of thy best knights to fight with spear or sword, horse or foot. If we win, Lady Guinevere shall be mine along with three of thy castles."

A herald blew the trumpet and the duke rode away. King Leodegrance's spirit fell. His heart was heavy. "It is doubtful another knight such as the White Champion will defend me. I don't know where he came from or where he went."

The king worried throughout the night. The next day, as promised, the duke and his knights appeared in front of the castle. Each knight rode a noble horse. Behind them, seven esquires followed bearing spears, shields, crests, and banners of his master. In front of the knights rode seven heralds with trumpets.

When the seven heralds blew their trumpets, a great crowd gathered to see the spectacle. The court of King Ryence came and stood upon the plain in front of the king's pavilion. They shouted and cheered for the Duke of North Umber and his six knights.

Meanwhile, King Leodegrance felt shame. He refused to show his face. Nevertheless, Lady Guinevere knocked upon his door. "My Lord, cheer up. I do believe the White Champion will return by day's end and overthrow our enemies."

She was correct. At sunset, a great cloud of dust appeared in the distance. And in that dust were five knights riding at great speed. Leading them was the White Champion!

The four knights with the White Champion were famous and brave knights. They were Sir Gawaine, Sir Ewaine, Sir Geraint, and Sir Pellias. There were no finer knights in all the land.

The people of the castle knew and loved these knights. Their hearts swelled with pride at the sight of them. Shouts of adoration caused King Leodegrance to come to the window with Lady Guinevere.

Upon seeing the White Champion and his knights, Lady Guinevere's heart filled with joy. She wept and waved her kerchief to the noble lords and kissed her hand to each one. The knights saluted her as they rode into the field. They were prepared to protect her honor.

The Duke of North Umber came forth from the pavilion. He spoke to the White Champion, "Sir Knight, no one knows thee.

Yesterday, I didn't ask who thou were and didn't know how thee would conduct thyself in battle. But now this quarrel is more serious. I won't allow my knights to battle with thee until thy identity is known."

Sir Gawaine took off his helmet and bowed his head. "I am Sir Gawaine, the son of King Lot. Know that I am more esteemed than thy own. The White Knight, I assure you, is of even better quality. That's all thee need know."

"There is another reason," said the duke, "that we may not fight with thee. We are seven famous knights and thou are but five. It is unequal. It would be too dangerous to thee."

Sir Gawaine smiled grimly upon the Duke of North Umber. "Thou shows tenderness concerning our safety. But I consider thy seven equal to our five. A simple man observing would be more concerned for thy safety."

Although the duke did not want to battle, he felt embarrassed by Sir Gawaine's words. So, each knight closed his helmet and rode to his end of the field. Then King Arthur and Duke Mordaunt each shouted aloud and one party hurled upon the other. The ground shook beneath the hooves of the horses. Clouds of dust rose up against the heavens.

When one party passed the other and the dust cleared, three of the seven had been overthrown. Not one of the five had lost his seat. One of the knights overthrown was the duke. For King Arthur had directed his spear in the middle of his shield. It pierced and killed Duke Mordaunt instantly. The world was rid of an evil man!

King Arthur turned to the knights and said, "My adventure is now done. It is now four against four—a fair and even match. I shall watch thee defeat our enemy from here."

The knights quickly overcame the knights from North Umber. They were welcomed into the gates of Cameliard with cheers and shouts from the people. As the knights rode in, one was missing—the White Champion!

# CHAPTER
## 11

# *The Round Table*

By the next morning, King Ryence had struck down his pavilions. He had withdrawn his court and left nothing behind. With him, he took the body of the Duke of North Umber.

When the people of Cameliard saw he was gone, they rejoiced. Not understanding that a growing flame of anger grew inside King Ryence, they sang and laughed.

At noon that day, a messenger appeared before King Leodegrance. "My lord King, let it be known that my master, King Ryence of North Wales, is displeased with thee. Thy knights have killed an excellent nobleman. Now King Ryence has two conditions. First, deliver the White Knight who killed the duke to him. Second, all lands in question must be delivered to King Ryence at once."

King Leodegrance rose from his seat. "The duke died because of his pride. I would not deliver the White Knight to thee even if I were able. As for the land he demands? Tell thy master that I will not deliver as much as a blade of grass to him."

The messenger spoke again. "If that is thy answer, then know that King Ryence will come forth with a great army and take what he wants." With those words, he departed.

King Leodegrance summoned Lady Guinevere. "A knight clad all in white with no crest has come to our rescue twice. I hear he is thy champion and wore thy necklace in battle. Tell me who he is. Where can he be found?"

"I don't know who he is," said Lady Guinevere. "But it seems that the gardener's boy knows more about the White Champion than anybody in the world. If thou sends for the gardener's boy, thee may get thy answer."

A page brought the gardener's boy to the king. With him came Sir Gawaine, Sir Ewaine, Sir Pellias, and Sir Geraint. King Leodegrance spoke to the gardener's boy. "Why would thee wear thy cap in my presence?"

"I cannot take it off," said the boy.

Lady Guinevere stepped forward. "I beseech thee to take thy cap off for my father."

As soon as the boy took his cap off, King Leodegrance recognized him. "My Lord and my King! What is this?" He knelt down before King Arthur. "Have thee done all these wonderful things for me?"

King Arthur stooped and kissed King Leodegrance upon the cheek. "It was I."

Lady Guinevere trembled. "I have mocked thee in the yard." She hung her head. "I am afraid of thy greatness."

"I am afraid of thee," said King Arthur. "I have thought of thee each day since thee stood above me in the hermit's house. I have served in the garden to see you and be in your goodwill."

"Thou have my goodwill," said Lady Guinevere. "In great measure."

He kissed her in front of all gathered.

Sir Kay and Sir Ulfius had gathered a great army as King Arthur asked them to do. When King Ryence came against Cameliard, he was easily defeated. His army quickly dispersed. King Ryence was chased into the mountains.

There was great rejoicing in Cameliard. After his victory, King Arthur remained there with a splendid court of noble lords. There was daily feasting and jousting and many famous bouts of arms. King Arthur and Lady Guinevere were very happy together and would soon marry.

⚜

One day King Leodegrance asked King Arthur, "My Lord, what shall I offer thee for a dowry when my daughter becomes thy queen?"

King Arthur turned to Merlin. "What shall I demand of my friend by way of dowry?"

Merlin's eyes sparkled. "Let me tell thee a story. In the days of thy father, Uther-Pendragon, I made a table for him. It was in the shape of a ring, so men called it the Round Table. There were fifty seats. It was designed for the fifty most worthy knights in the world. Whenever such a knight appeared, his name would appear in gold letters upon his seat. When he died, his name would vanish.

"Forty-nine of these seats were the same. One was set aside for the king himself. It was elevated above the others and was called the Seat Perilous. When Uther-Pendragon died, the table was given to his good friend King Leodegrance.

"In the beginning of King Leodegrance's reign, twenty-four knights sat at the table. But times have changed. Many knights deserted King Leodegrance. His is the only name that appears now. If thee gets the table as a dowry then it will lend itself to glory. The knights who sit there will be the best and never forgotten."

"If that shall bring thee great glory," said King Leodegrance, "then it will bring me glory and thy renown shall also be mine."

So King Arthur became the master of the famous Round Table. The table was set up at Camelot and the knights that sat there were the best. This is the history of the beginning of the Round Table.

# A Royal Wedding

Fall came upon Camelot. It was this season in which King Arthur would marry his love, Lady Guinevere. All the world was joyful that the king was to have a queen. It was a moment they had waited for with anticipation.

Preparations were under way. The street along which Lady Guinevere would travel to the royal castle was decorated. Many grand carpets lined the streets. Flags and banners blew in the gentle breeze. To onlookers, the world was alive with bright colors.

"King Arthur, thy lady has arrived," said a messenger.

King Arthur's heart fluttered. Never before had he felt such love for anyone. He rose with great joy and traveled down the street with his court. As he walked, shouts filled the air.

When he came upon Lady Guinevere in her carriage, he placed one hand beneath her chin. He kissed her cheek. The crowd that had gathered roared with delight.

When high noon came, the two were led to the cathedral where the archbishop married them. All the bells rang joyfully and there was a feast for all. There was much celebrating to be had.

And that day was very famous in the history of chivalry. For in the afternoon, the famous Round Table was established. It would be the crowning glory of King Arthur's reign.

Merlin led King Arthur and his queen into a pavilion. It appeared to be a magical room, for the walls were richly gilded. Upon them were drawings of saints and angels playing musical instruments. It was a sight to behold.

In the middle of the pavilion was the Round Table with seats for exactly fifty people. At each place was a chalice of gold filled with wine. Next to each chalice was a gold bowl that held bread.

"What a wondrous sight," said King Arthur to Merlin. "What a wondrous day."

Merlin pointed to the high seat. "Behold, my lord King, thy seat is that one." And as he spoke, *Arthur, King* suddenly appeared in gold upon the back of his seat.

"Thou are the center seat, my master."

Then Merlin pointed to the seat opposite of King Arthur's. "That is called the Seat Perilous. For no one that is already born upon this earth may sit there. To do so would mean death or terrible misfortune. It shall be filled one day."

"Merlin," said King Arthur, "I beseech thee to fill up each seat now so the Round Table will be complete."

Merlin sighed. "Why are thee in such a hurry? Know that when this Round Table is entirely filled, thy entire glory will have been achieved. Then, thy decline begins because thy work will be done. Therefore, I cannot fill each seat now. Your work is not yet finished and won't be for some time."

Merlin paused to look at the Round Table. "Though thee has gathered the most noble of men, only thirty-two are considered worthy to sit at the Round Table."

"Then choose my thirty-two right away," said King Arthur. "Why wait any longer?"

And Merlin did. King Pellinore was chosen to sit at the left hand of the Royal Seat. Next came Sir Gawaine and Sir Ewaine, then Sir Kay, Sir Baudwain, and Sir Pellias. It continued until thirty-two noble knights had been seated.

When all had been chosen, King Arthur asked why the seat upon his right hand had not been filled. "Merlin, how is this? Why is there no name here?"

"Lord, there shall be a name soon. And he who sits there shall be the greatest knight in all the world. That is, of course, until a knight comes to occupy the Seat Perilous."

The Archbishop of Canterbury blessed every seat. As he blessed each one, the chosen knight's esquire stood behind his knight's head holding his coat of arms upon the spear point. And all those who stood about would cheer for the knight.

Then all the knights rose and took an oath. This was the Covenant of the Knighthood of the Round Table. They promised to be gentle to the weak, courageous to the strong, hold all women in the highest regard, be merciful to all men, gentle in deed, true in friendship, and faithful in love.

More celebrating followed as each drank wine and broke bread while giving thanks to God for all he had given them. This was truly a great day for Merlin, King Arthur, and Queen Guinevere—and for all of the Knights of the Round Table.

# Morgana's Evil Plan

Queen Morgana le Fay wasn't happy with King Arthur's Round Table. She was furious that her brother had passed over her son, Sir Baudemagus.

"My sister, I am sorry that thee are not pleased with my selection. But I assure thee I did what was best for my power. It is my honest belief that others are more worthy."

She despised his every word.

Now Morgana le Fay was a cunning enchantress. Merlin himself had been her master and taught her much of what she knew. She became bitter and believed she could never again be happy unless she could punish King Arthur. She wanted him dead.

But Queen Morgana knew she could never cause King Arthur harm as long as Merlin protected him. For Merlin could foresee all danger to the king. In order to destroy the king, she had to first destroy Merlin.

In her court there was a young girl of just fifteen. She was the daughter of King Northumberland. Her name was Vivien. She was wise and cunning beyond her years. She was heartless, cold, and cruel to all who didn't share her thoughts.

Queen Morgana liked her and taught her the ways of magic and sorcery. But no matter how hard she tried, Queen Morgana knew that Vivien disliked her.

One day, they were sitting in the garden on the magic island of Avalon when Morgana came up with a plan. "Vivien, what do thee want most in this world?"

"I wish to have thy wisdom, Queen Morgana."

Queen Morgana laughed. "I know a way that thee may obtain as much wisdom as me. Merlin taught me all that I know of magic. There are, however, many things he withheld. Merlin has the gift of seeing the future. But while he can see the fate of others, he's blind to his own fate."

Vivien held her breath.

"Thou are far more beautiful that I was at thy age. Merlin will be attracted to thee. And if I add a charm, Merlin will love thee so much that he will impart a great deal more of his wisdom on thee than he did to me."

Vivien listened with great interest. "When I've drawn all the knowledge that I can from Merlin, I'll use that same knowledge to cast a spell upon him. He shall never be able to harm me or anyone else again. I shall play my wit against his wisdom and my beauty against his cunning ways. I believe I shall win this game."

Queen Morgana laughed. "I believe thou are as wicked as thou are cunning." She lifted a small ivory whistle to her lips and blew upon it. Three pages ran forth carrying a box.

Opening the box, Queen Morgana took out two gold rings. One had a stone as red as blood. The other had a stone of clear white brilliance.

"These two rings possess a spell. If thee wears the white stone, whoever wears the red stone shall love thee. He will do as thy ask, for his love will be so great. Now take these to King Arthur's court. Use the rings wisely."

At this time in King Arthur's court, a great feast was prepared for Pentecost. The king liked to have entertainment at such feasts. As the court enjoyed the merriment, a beautiful girl walked into the room.

"Who art thou?" asked King Arthur.

"I am Vivien, the daughter of King Northumberland." As she was of royal blood, King Arthur was satisfied. "I seek to give thee entertainment during this feast. For here is a ring that only the most wise and worthy of men may wear." She held the ring up for all to see.

"May I put the ring on my finger?" asked the king.

Vivien stepped forward. "It would be an honor." But before placing it on his finger, it grew smaller. It would not go past the first joint.

"It would appear I am not worthy," said King Arthur, amused. "Offer it to others."

This is exactly what Vivien wanted to do. As she took the ring to each nobleman, the ring didn't fit. Until she came to Merlin, that is. It slipped on his finger with ease.

"Thou are the most wise and worthy," said Vivien.

Merlin looked at the young girl and wondered if trickery was involved. He tried to take the ring off but couldn't!

As he tugged, the spell deepened. He suddenly noticed Vivien's beauty and took great pleasure in it. Many saw the sparkle in Merlin's eye when he looked at the girl. Many said, "Merlin is bewitched by the beauty of that girl."

Indeed this was true. No matter where Vivien went, Merlin followed. If she was in the garden, Merlin was with her. If she entered the great hall, it was certain Merlin would enter next. This was too much for Vivien. She often tried to escape him.

"Do thee hate me, Vivien?" asked Merlin. "I would do anything for thy love."

"Sir, I do not hate thee." Vivien wasn't telling the truth. "But if thou imparts thy wisdom onto me, I would have more love for thee. Thou are so wise that I am afraid of thee. Teach me thy cunning ways and I'll grow to regard thee as thee regards me."

Merlin knew that teaching her everything he knew would lead to his downfall. But, his heart got the best of him.

"I will teach thee but not in this place. I can only teach in solitude so no one disturbs us. Go to King Arthur and tell him that thee must return to thy father's kingdom. Then we'll depart together with thy court. We will then travel. I'll build a place for us to stay while I instruct thee."

Vivien was joyful. She grabbed Merlin's hand and kissed it.

If Merlin could foresee his future, he would have known the doom that lay ahead.

# CHAPTER
## 14

# Merlin's Fate

Merlin, Vivien, and her court traveled for three days before coming to a dark forest. "I will now use my magic," Merlin said. "Stand aside and I shall show thee what I can do." All became quiet.

Minutes later, Merlin's magic was evident. A grand castle appeared before their eyes. It was a sight of great glory. "I give you this castle, Vivien, as a sign of my devotion to you."

Vivien was pleased. Knowing Merlin was under her spell was of great comfort to her. "Master, will thou teach me things such as this so I can build my own castle?"

"I will teach thee much more than that," Merlin said, staring into Vivien's beautiful face.

"I shall teach charms and spells that will amaze thee." He took her hand. "Do thee still hate me, Vivien?" He held his breath waiting for the answer. He wanted so much for her to love him as much as he loved her.

She kissed his hand. "No. I do not hate you, my fair Merlin." But she didn't speak the truth. For in her heart she was evil. The heart of Merlin was good. That which is evil will always hate that which is good.

Although she spoke lovingly, Vivien hated Merlin because of his great wisdom. She despised him and his generous ways. The only reason Merlin loved her was because of the ring. Vivien knew this and it made her more determined to rid the world of him once and for all.

After a year in the castle, Merlin announced, "Vivien, I have taught thee all I know. No one knows more magic at this time. I have no more power than thee. We are equal in power."

Vivien was overjoyed. The next day, she prepared a feast to celebrate. She also prepared a sleeping potion for Merlin. "Sir, drink from this chalice and celebrate with me."

Since Merlin suspected no evil, he sipped from the cup. Suddenly, Merlin's thoughts became cloudy. At once, he knew he was betrayed.

"Woe is me! I am betrayed! Woe is me!" He tried to rise up but couldn't. "Why betray me, my beautiful Vivien?"

Vivien smiled at him. She set another spell upon Merlin causing him to remain motionless. He was trapped.

"Behold, Merlin! Thou are now in my power. Thou cannot move a single hair without me. I have used the enchantments thee taught me against thyself. All thy power is now my power."

Merlin groaned. "Thou have shamed me. Even if released from this spell, I could never

let any man see my face again. But now, I have one favor I must ask of you."

Vivien listened closely.

"I have gained my gift of foresight once again," Merlin continued. "I see that King Arthur is in great danger. His life is at stake. Please use thy powers and save him. By fulfilling this one good deed, thee will lessen the sin of betraying me."

Vivien was evil, but she still felt a small amount of pity for Merlin and had a slight reverence for King Arthur.

"Very well," she said. "I shall do it."

Merlin told her to go into the West Country into a castle of Sir Domas de Noir. "Thou will know what must be done."

Vivien then used her magic to place Merlin in a sealed coffin. She placed a slab upon the coffin. Merlin lay beneath it like one who was dead.

Vivien then caused the castle to disappear and leave no trace behind. She quickly left the valley with a feeling of great joy that she had triumphed over Merlin. Nevertheless, she kept her promise and walked toward the castle of Sir Domas de Noir.

As for Merlin, he was never seen or heard from again.

# CHAPTER 15

# Morgana's Trickery Continues

Queen Morgana le Fay returned to Camelot and kneeled before the king. "Brother, I have talked ill against thee and I am sorry. Please forgive my evil words."

King Arthur was moved. "My sister, I have no ill will against thee. I have only love in my heart for thee." King Arthur was happy they were reconciled.

One day, King Arthur and Queen Morgana started to talk about Excalibur. Queen Morgana expressed a great desire to see the weapon up close. The king took the sword and handed it to her. "Take it and keep it for as long as thee wish."

Queen Morgana had never seen anything so beautiful! She took the sword and its sheath and hid them in her bed. Then she sent for the best armorsmiths, goldsmiths, and jewelers.

"Make me a sword identical to this one," she demanded.

In two weeks, they returned a sword that looked so much like Excalibur, no one could tell the difference between the two.

A few weeks later, King Arthur ordered a hunt for his knights. Queen Morgana presented him with a noble horse.

"My sister, never have I seen a finer horse," said King Arthur. "I shall ride it forth upon the hunt tomorrow. I consider it a gift of forgiveness between us." King Arthur had no reason to question such a gift.

During the hunt, the king and his court followed chase with great eagerness. But the horse of King Arthur soon outran all others except for Sir Accalon. So the two rode together through the forest.

It wasn't long before they got lost in the thick forest. King Arthur's horse continued along a certain path while Sir Accalon followed.

At last, they emerged from the forest. Before them was a beach of smooth sand. As they looked out to sea, they saw a ship. It was painted many bright colors. Its sails were of silk cloth.

It wasn't long before the ship beached upon the shore. The two rode forth to inspect the ship. As they approached, twelve beautiful damsels in rich scarlet garments appeared.

"Welcome, King Arthur! Welcome, Sir Accalon!"

King Arthur was astonished when they knew his name. "Fair ladies, thou appear to know me but I do not know of thee."

The chief damsel replied, "We are part fairy, and we know all about thee. Thee have been following a long chase and are hungry and tired. Come aboard and refresh with food and drink."

The ladies lowered the gangplank. King Arthur and Sir Accalon went to them.

After resting and eating, the ladies offered King Arthur a place to sleep. They led Sir Accalon to another resting spot. King Arthur felt such comfort that he quickly fell asleep.

When King Arthur awoke the next day, something was wrong. He was in a dungeon surrounded by sad voices.

"Where is the ship I was on? Where are the ladies?" he asked.

He looked around the room filled with twenty-two knights. One spoke, "Sir, we are all prisoners in the dungeon of this castle. It belongs to Sir Domas, a knight. Last night, two men in black brought thee here as prisoner."

"Tell me," said King Arthur, "who is this Sir Domas? I have never heard of him."

The knight spoke softly, "He is the foulest knight on earth with the heart of a coward. Yet he is a powerful man in these parts. He has a brother, Sir Ontzlake. When their father died, he left each one an equal share in his estates. But Sir Domas has taken much of Sir Ontzlake's land. He left him with just one castle. Now he wants that one as well. He will stop at nothing to get it."

"What does Sir Ontzlake do to stop this?" asked King Arthur.

"Sir Ontzlake is a brave and courageous knight. Sir Domas is afraid to attempt battle with him for he knows he will lose. So for a long time, Sir Domas has searched for a knight to battle his brother. He brings us here and gives us a choice to remain in this place forever or fight his brother. None of us here will battle for him."

King Arthur stood. "If he asks me, I shall fight for him. I would rather do battle than be a prisoner here forever. Then after the battle, I will fight Sir Domas."

At that moment, a young lady opened the door. "Sir, I am sorry to see so noble a knight here. But if you'll defend the cause of the lord of this castle, thee may leave."

"Lady, I will undertake thy adventure. If I should win, these fine knights shall go forth in freedom," Arthur answered.

"Very well," said the lady.

King Arthur looked closely at this woman. "Haven't I seen thee before today?"

"No, sir. I am the daughter of this castle. It couldn't be." This was false. She was the one who beckoned King Arthur onto the ship and delivered him to Sir Domas. All of these things were done at the command of Morgana le Fay.

"If I battle, thou must carry a message to the court of King Arthur. Deliver my message to Queen Morgana le Fay."

The damsel agreed.

So King Arthur wrote a letter asking Queen Morgana to send Excalibur to him. When she received the letter, she laughed and sent him the other sword she had made—the sword with no powers.

# A Battle Between Friends

When Sir Accalon awoke from his sleep, he found himself lying near a large pavilion. Immediately, he knew this was the result of an evil spell.

"God save King Arthur from harm," he said. He then walked over to the pavilion. A woman was sitting at the center of a table.

"Sir, will thou sit down with me? I am Lady Gomyne of the Fair Hair. Come and feast."

Sir Accalon was starved and sat with the beauty.

"Sir, thou appears to be a strong and worthy lord. One used to battle," she said.

"I've engaged in several battles. I believe my enemies would tell thee that I am most worthy."

"There is a worthy knight here that is in need of thy services," said Lady Gomyne. The lady told him all about her master, Sir Ontzlake, and his evil brother, Sir Domas. "Word has come that Sir Domas has found himself a worthy champion of great strength and prowess. Sir Ontzlake cannot fight due to an injury caused by a spear."

"Lady, I would be honored to defend Sir Ontzlake's right," said Sir Accalon. "But I have no armor to do battle."

Upon this she rose and went to the field. She brought back a scarlet cloth. She opened the cloth before Sir Accalon's eyes. In the cloth was Excalibur in its sheath!

"This sword shall be thy own if thee assumes the battle upon behalf of Sir Ontzlake."

When Sir Accalon held the sword, he was confused. "This is either Excalibur or its twin brother. This sword is just like one I've set my eyes on before."

"I have heard," said the lady, "that there is another sword like this."

"To win this sword, I am willing to partake in battle."

"If the battle is won, thee may keep this sword for thyself."

Sir Accalon rejoiced at the thought of making that sword his own.

He would not have rejoiced if he knew that Morgana le Fay had worked her cunning charms on him. Through her, King Arthur was to battle a knight beloved by him. And that knight had Excalibur to use against his master!

A field was prepared for battle. Each knight was given arms and a good steed. King Arthur was clad in armor of Sir Domas. Sir Accalon wore Sir Ontzlake's armor. Each wore a helmet over his head so he couldn't see the other's face.

Word was given and the two rushed forth with speed and fury. They met in the middle with a roar of thunder. The spear of each knight burst into small pieces. The knights allowed their horses to run free as they landed on foot and drew swords. Once again, they charged each other.

At this time, Vivien, upon Merlin's last request, came to see the battle. As she looked at the knights, she couldn't tell which was King Arthur and which was his enemy.

As they approached with swords, the sword of Sir Accalon bit deeply into King Arthur. He was wounded! Blood gushed from him. Although the sword of King Arthur touched Sir Accalon's armor, no harm came to him due to the sheath of Excalibur.

When King Arthur realized all the blood on the ground was his and not a drop came from his enemy, he feared he'd die in battle. "Is it possible that the sword I have is not Excalibur but the one of my enemy is?"

With a gasp, King Arthur struck Sir Accalon with his sword. In doing so, the sword broke. Sir Accalon ran toward King Arthur. "Thou have lost a great deal of blood and are now without weapon. Yield thyself to me."

"Nay, Sir Knight," said King Arthur. "I cannot bring shame to myself. I'd rather die with honor."

"Then I must strike a final blow," said Sir Accalon. As he lifted Excalibur over King Arthur, Vivien struck her hands in great force together. It appeared that Sir Accalon received a forceful blow to his arm. Excalibur fell out of his hands and onto the grass.

Then King Arthur saw the sword—his sword. "Treason!" he yelled. "Who betrayed me?" He knelt on the sword. And as he did, it appeared that a great rage came to King Arthur. He raised the sword and struck Sir Accalon over and over.

Sir Accalon fell down upon his knees. King Arthur ran forward and plucked away the sheath from his hands. When he did this, the wounds of Sir Accalon burst out bleeding.

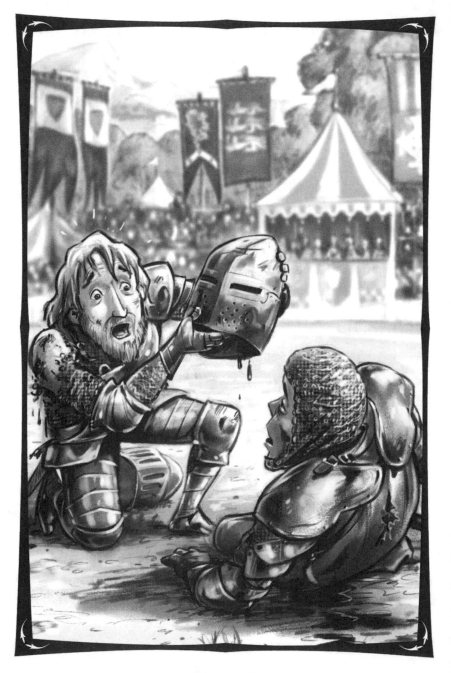

"Sir Knight, why have thee betrayed me?" asked King Arthur.

"I have not betrayed thee," gasped Sir Accalon. "I am a knight in good standing with King Arthur's court."

King Arthur could not believe these words. "Do thee know who I am?" demanded King Arthur.

"I do not," said Sir Accalon. It was then that King Arthur took off his helmet. "I am thy master." King Arthur took off his enemy's helmet and couldn't believe it was Sir Accalon.

When all gathered saw that King Arthur was among them, they ran out into the field. Vivien came forth and used her powers to heal King Arthur's wounds.

When the king asked her to save Sir Accalon, she lied and said, "I cannot, for I have no more healing balsam."

So that afternoon, Sir Accalon died of his battle wounds.

King Arthur summoned both Sir Domas and Sir Ontzlake into his presence. They trembled in terror.

"I will pardon thee, Sir Ontzlake, for thee know not what thee did. But Sir Domas, thee are a treasonable and evil knight. I will take all of thy possessions but one castle and give them to thy brother. Thee may no longer ride upon any horse. For thee are not worthy to ride like a true knight. Thou must free all those in thy dungeon at once."

He dismissed the two knights, who were very glad that King Arthur showed them such mercy.

# Forever Gone

Shortly after the battle, word reached Morgana le Fay that King Arthur defeated Sir Accalon. "How can it be that my spell did not work? What could have gone wrong?"

Queen Morgana worried that King Arthur might know of her treasonous ways. She decided to find him and beg forgiveness. So she gathered her court and traveled to him.

She found him five days after the battle took place. When she arrived she asked those in charge about King Arthur.

"He is asleep and resting. He is not to be disturbed."

"I am not to be forbidden," said Queen Morgana. "I am his sister. He would never allow me to travel this far and return home. I demand to speak to him at once."

Queen Morgana was allowed entrance into King Arthur's sleeping chamber. She crept in and didn't dare make a noise to awaken him. As she watched him sleep, she was filled with hate and rage. So much so that she knew she had to destroy him.

"I'll take Excalibur and his shield and bring them to Avalon. My brother shall never see them again."

She saw that the king had Excalibur beside him. As he slept, his hand held the handle of the sword. She hesitated and thought, *If I try to take Excalibur from his hand and he awakens, he will slay me for my treason.*

That's when she spied the sheath of Excalibur at the foot of the couch. So she took the sheath and slipped out of the room while King Arthur remained in a deep sleep.

When she left the chamber, she said to all, "Do not waken the king." Then she mounted her horse and fled.

When King Arthur woke, he noticed his sheath was missing. "Where is the sheath for Excalibur? Who has been in this room?"

"Queen Morgana le Fay has been in thy presence. She didn't want to wake thee from sleep," said an attendant.

"I feel she has used her cunning ways on me from the beginning to the end of these adventures," said King Arthur. He summoned all the knights and esquires and they pursued Queen Morgana. Despite how ill and faint he felt, Arthur led the way.

As he was ready to depart, Vivien came to him. "Take me with thee, my Lord. If thou do not, the sheath of Excalibur will not be recovered. Thou will never be able to overtake the wicked Queen Morgana le Fay."

King Arthur agreed to take Vivien. He was grateful for her help.

As Queen Morgana fled, she looked behind her. She could see that Vivien was with King Arthur. Her heart was heavy.

"I fear that I'm ruined," Morgana said. "For I have aided that damsel and helped her acquire her magic. I have no spells left to save myself from her cunning ways. But at least I know that King Arthur will never have the sheath of Excalibur again to help him."

At this time, Queen Morgana passed by a lake. She took the sheath of Excalibur and swung it above her head. Then, she threw it out into the water.

Before Morgana's eyes, a miracle occurred! A woman's arm rose out of the water. It was dressed in white. The hand caught the sheath of Excalibur and drew it under water. No one ever laid eyes on the sheath again.

After Morgana threw the sheath into the lake, she went on farther to where stones and rocks lay upon the coast. She used all the spells

Merlin had taught her to turn herself, her court, and their horses into rock and stones.

As King Arthur approached the rocky area, Vivien said, "Those stones are Queen Morgana and her court. She's used Merlin's magic to disguise them. I can remove the magic. If I do, thee must promise to punish that wicked woman by killing her instantly."

The king looked upon Vivien with great displeasure. "Damsel, thou hasn't suffered injury at the hands of Queen Morgana. So then why would thee have me slay her? I forgive her of all this. I shall forgive her again and again if she sins against me, for her mother was my mother. The blood which flows in her veins and in my veins is from the same fountain. Therefore, I will do no evil against her."

Vivien looked at King Arthur with disgust. "Thou are a fool!" Then she vanished. Because King Arthur had rebuked her for her wickedness in front of others, she hated him even more than Morgana le Fay had hated him.

King Arthur learned how Vivien had tricked him. He felt great sadness that Merlin too was tricked by such an evil person.

King Arthur gazed out over the lake. He knew his sheath was lost forever. He grieved this loss, for he knew that it would surely mean the end of him sometime soon.

Soon enough, it did mean the end of King Arthur's reign as many rose up to challenge him. Without the sheath to protect him, he was wounded.

Some say that his wounds were the end of him and he died a violent death. Still, others say that King Arthur never died after battle. Instead, he was taken to the magical island of Avalon by the Sea. It was there that he recovered from his wounds. He still waits there for his grand return to his throne.

When and if he returns, Merlin's prophecy of Arthur being "The Once and Future King" will be fulfilled.